King for a Day

Thomishia Booker

CHILDREN'S BOOK SERIES

Copyright © 2017 Thomishia Booker

ISBN-13: 978-1-7339159-1-5

This book is sold subject to the condition that it shall not, by way of trade or otherwise, be lent, resold, hired out or otherwise circulated without the publisher's prior consent in any form of binding or cover other than that in which it is published and without a similar condition including this condition being imposed on the subsequent publisher.
The moral right of the author has been asserted.

Illustrations Copyright © Thomishia Booker

Illustration and Book Design by Uzuri Designs
www.uzuridesignsbooks.com

King for a Day

Thomishia Booker

Illustrated by Jessica Gibson & Vicky Amrullah

If I were King for a day

Here's what I'd do

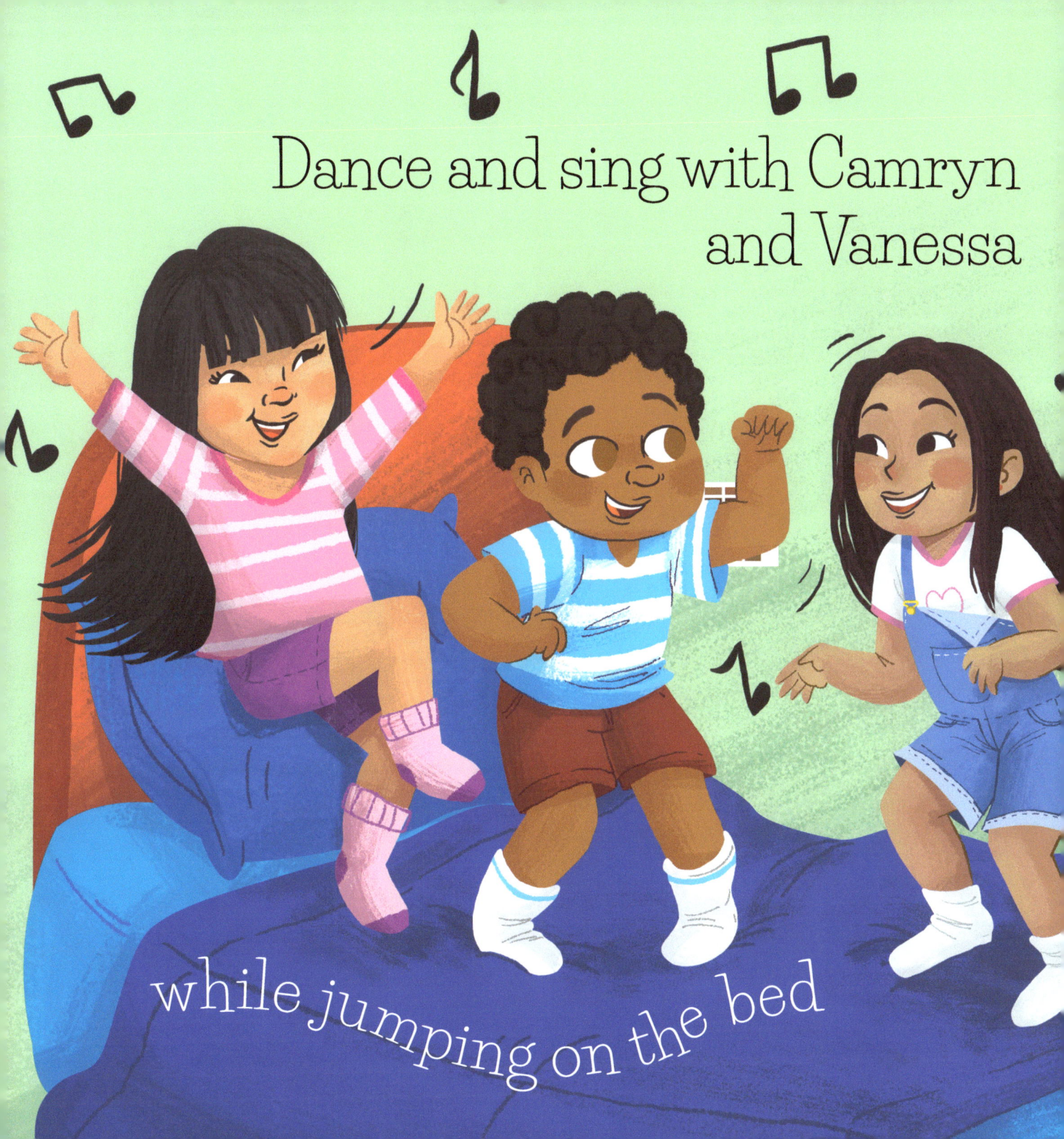

I would fly to school every day so I wouldn't be late

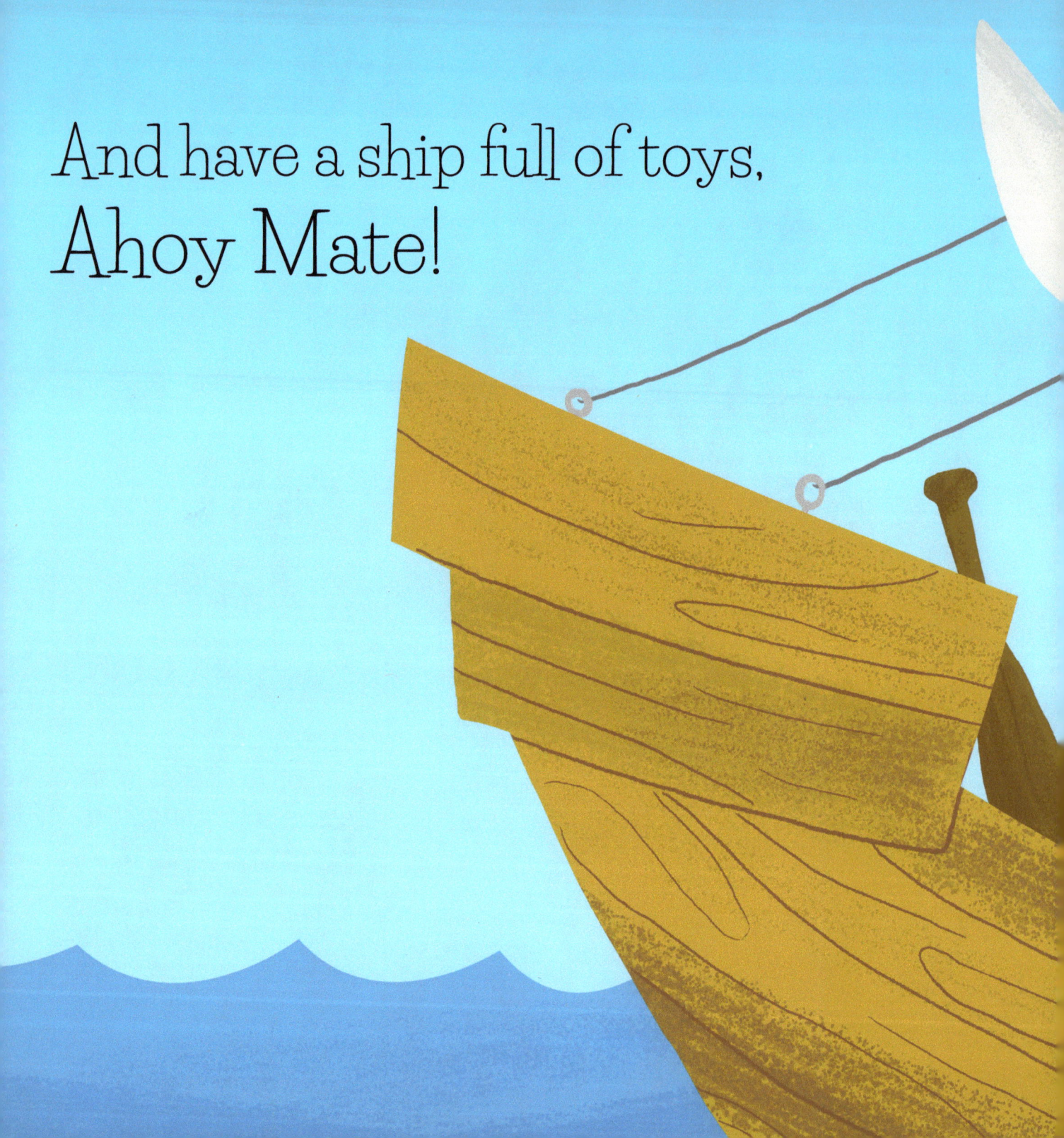
And have a ship full of toys, Ahoy Mate!

Have ice cream for dinner and my mom would never ask why

Eric and Noelan would always come over to play
I'd make them my brothers if I were King for a day!

I'd be a fair King, tried and true

Dress up like my dad and go to work,
Yeah that's what I'd do!

If I were King for a day, it would be so much fun

I'd make all my dreams come true before the day was done!

Daily Affirmations Activity

Engage your child in a conversation about their talents. Write them on pieces of paper and place them around the house.

Repeat after me!

I am smart!
I am loved!
I am amazing!
I am wonderful!
I can do anything!

CPSIA information can be obtained
at www.ICGtesting.com
Printed in the USA
LVHW070601301220
675396LV00034B/2002